THE CARDBOARD KINGDOM
ROAR OF THE BEAST

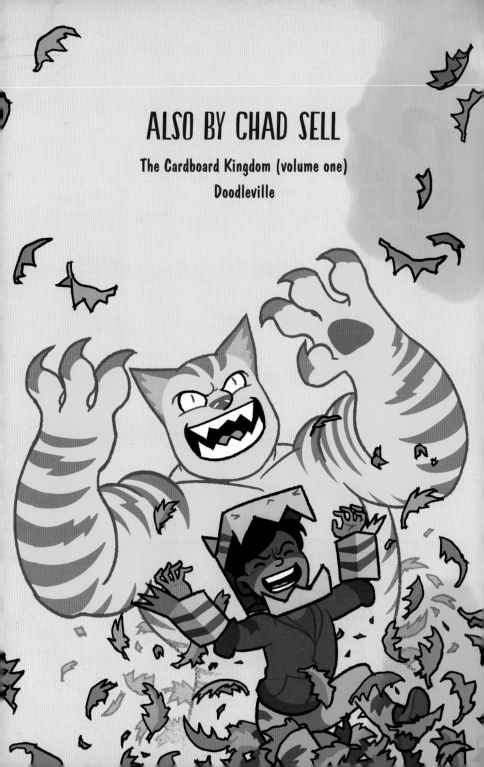

ALSO BY CHAD SELL

The Cardboard Kingdom (volume one)
Doodleville

THE CARDBOARD KINGDOM

ROAR OF THE BEAST

ART BY
CHAD SELL

STORY BY

Chad Sell, Vid Alliger, Manuel Betancourt,
Michael Cole, David DeMeo, Jay Fuller, Cloud Jacobs,
Barbara Perez Marquez, Molly Muldoon,
and Katie Schenkel

ALFRED A. KNOPF ⟋⟍ NEW YORK

THE SCIENCE SQUAD

THE ANIMAL QUEEN AND HER "CAPTAIN OF THE GUARD"

THE GREATEST CARDBOARD CRAFTERS IN THE KINGDOM

THE OWNERS OF THE DRAGON'S HEAD INN

WHAT IS ALICE UP TO??

THE DRAGON'S HEAD INN

OKAY, THAT'S 25 GOLD FOR EACH.

HEY...

WHY ARE YOU... DRAWING **NEW** COSTUMES?

YOU ALREADY **HAVE** COSTUMES.

BUT THESE ARE GOING TO BE **HALLOWEEN** COSTUMES!

FOR TRICK-OR-TREATING!

WE MUST BE SUFFICIENTLY TERRIFYING SO THAT THE HUMANS GIVE US ALL THEIR CANDY.

EXACTLY!

IT'S NOT A **BAD** THING, ALICE!

I **LOVE** SCARY STUFF!

IT'S TRUE. SHE WATCHES THE GROSSEST, GORIEST HORROR MOVIES.

YOU COULD BE A **MONSTER** IN ONE OF **THOSE**, ALICE.

I'LL... TAKE THAT AS A **COMPLIMENT**.

ALICE, WE'RE ON OUR LAST BATCH OF CINNEMAGIC CIDER.

ALICE?

ARE YOU **OKAY**?

IS SOMETHING **WRONG**?

WHAT?

OH, I JUST HAD AN IDEA SO **GOOD**... IT'S **SCARY**!

MWAHAHAHA!

UH-OH.

DO YOU HAVE PLANS FOR HALLOWEEN, YOUR MAJESTY?

OR IS TRICK-OR-TREATING ONLY FOR... **PEASANTS**?

NO, IT'S FOR QUEENS, TOO.

BUT MOMMY AND DADDY DON'T MAKE IT MUCH **FUN**.

ARE THEY... A LITTLE PROTECTIVE?

A **LITTLE**? I CANNOT WALK DOWN THE **DRIVEWAY** WITHOUT THEM **WORRYING**!

I WISH I COULD JUST GO WITH **YOU**.

WELL, THAT SOUNDS GOOD TO **ME**!

WHY DON'T YOU ASK YOUR PARENTS?

SILENCE, BEAST!

HA HA! YOU **MISSED!**

THAT WAS A **WARNING SHOT.**

NOW GET **DOWN** FROM THERE OR FACE THE WRATH OF **ALICE.**

HEY, WHERE **IS** ALICE?

SHE WENT OFF **SCHEMING** SOMEWHERE.

AS USUAL.

I GUESS I'M LEFT TO CLEAN UP BY **MYSELF.**

AGAIN.

DON'T WORRY, BECKY!

WE CAN HELP!

"WE"?

PROXIMITY ALERT.

TEENAGERS APPROACHING.

ALERT! ALERT! CARDBOARD DORKS AHOY!

WHAT'VE YOU GOT THERE?

HEY! GIVE THAT BACK!

WHOA!

YOU'RE TRYING TO MAKE YOUR COSTUME EVEN **UGLIER**?

THAT'S QUITE A CHALLENGE.

HE **ASKED** YOU TO GIVE IT **BACK**!

GUYS...

RETURN THE SCHEMATIC OR RISK EXTERMINATION.

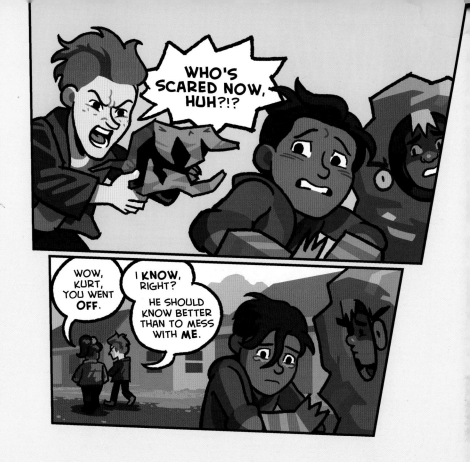

WHO'S SCARED NOW, HUH?!?

WOW, KURT, YOU WENT OFF.

I KNOW, RIGHT? HE SHOULD KNOW BETTER THAN TO MESS WITH ME.

19

GREETINGS, HUMAN.

WE HAVE RECOVERED THE CRUSHED COSTUME.

CAN WE HELP FIX IT?

WHAT **HAPPENED**?

WHO DID THIS?!

THE TEENAGE HUMAN.

KURT WAS PICKING ON ME, AND VIJAY STOOD UP TO HIM.

HE WAS REALLY BRAVE.

...BUT KURT PUSHED HIM AND SMASHED THE MASK.

WHAT?!

IS VIJAY GONNA BE OKAY?

I MEAN...

YEAH, OF COURSE.

I THINK.

WHY DIDN'T YOU **TELL ME** YOU GOT IN A FIGHT?

BECAUSE I **LOST**.

VIJAY, IT'S NOT...

YOU WERE JUST STANDING UP FOR YOUR **FRIEND**.

NEXT TIME, DON'T PICK A FIGHT WITH SOMEONE **BIGGER** THAN YOU.

OR...AT LEAST GET YOUR BIG SISTER FOR BACKUP.

I WON'T. I WON'T FIGHT **EVER** AGAIN.

ELIJAH AND CONNIE BROUGHT THIS.

THEY WANT TO HELP YOU FIX THE BEAST.

THAT'S **NOT** THE BEAST, SHIKHA.

THAT'S...

THAT'S JUST SOME **CARDBOARD**.

WHAT ARE **YOU** DOING HERE, ALICE?

ARE YOU **PLOTTING** SOMETHING?

ALICE WANTS TO SEE MY SCARY MOVIES! WE'RE--

STOP! THAT'S TOP-SECRET!

OH RIGHT, I'M NOT SUPPOSED TO SAY ANYTHING.

ALICE MADE ME SIGN AN **N.D.A.**

IT STANDS FOR "NONE OF YOUR DARN"...UH...

I DON'T **KNOW** WHAT IT STANDS FOR, BUT IT'S **SERIOUS**.

FINE.

BUT I'M **ALSO** WORKING ON SOMETHING SECRET!

SOMETHING SINISTER AND **SPECTACULAR**!

THAT'S NICE, DON'T CARE.

COME ON, SAM.

WHO EXACTLY ARE YOU TRYING TO IMPRESS?

HUH?

PICKING ON MY LITTLE BROTHER?

SMASHING HIS COSTUME?

DOES THAT MAKE YOU FEEL **TOUGH**, KURT?

I'M **NOT** TRYING TO IMPRESS **ANYBODY**.

I WAS **DEFENDING** MYSELF FROM YOUR **LITTLE MONSTER BROTHER**.

HOW **DARE** YOU?

UH-OH, BIG SISTER IS ENTERING **BEAST MODE!**

RARRR! HOW DARE AROOOO?!

HA HA!

STOP IT! OR...

NATE! YOU'RE UP!

ELI? HOW DID YOU ESCAPE?

FROM THE... THE **MONSTER**?

THE... WHAT?

THE THING THAT WAS ATTACKING YOU.

ATTACKING?

IN THE BACKYARD!

I WASN'T OUTSIDE, NATE. NOTHING **ATTACKED** ME.

BUT... I **SAW** IT.

I SHOULD PROBABLY GO GET MOM AND RODRIGO, BUT...

MAYBE DON'T MENTION THE MONSTER?

THEY'RE WORRIED **ENOUGH** AS IT IS.

NATE, ARE YOU OKAY?

I SAW **SOMETHING** ATTACKING HIM.

SOMETHING **BIG**.

BUT...

YOU DON'T BELIEVE ME?

WELL, MAYBE YOU SAW IT IN A **NIGHTMARE**, OR...?

I DON'T KNOW, NATE.

I KNOW WHAT I SAW.

THERE'S A **MONSTER** IN THE CARDBOARD KINGDOM.

THEN...

UH...

THEN THE TWO OF US WILL HUNT IT DOWN. **TOGETHER**.

ONCE YOUR LEG HEALS.

BUT WE CAN'T **WAIT** THAT LONG.

WHAT IF IT'S **STILL OUT THERE**?

WHAT IF **WHAT'S** STILL OUT THERE?

THE MONSTER
AND THE
STORM

IN THE EARLY AFTERNOON...

HEY, MIGUEL! IS NATE **OKAY?**

YEAH, IS HE HOME FROM THE HOSPITAL?

WHAT?

OH, **YEAH.**

I MEAN... **NO?**

HE'S NOT **OKAY,** BUT...

I HOPE HE **WILL** BE.

...ARE **YOU** OKAY?

ME??

UM, SURE, I GUESS.

TELL NATE HI FROM US, OKAY?

SURE, DEFINITELY.

WILL YOU COME BY THE DRAGON'S HEAD INN LATER?

WE'LL TRY!

HEY, SAM!

LET'S GO! SAM!

SAM?

HELLOOO?

HMM...

WHAT ARE **THEY** UP TO?

I WISH I KNEW.

THIS MONSTER STUFF REALLY BUGS YOU, HUH?

I GUESS.

I DON'T KNOW HOW TO FEEL ABOUT IT, EITHER.

I JUST HOPE THINGS GO BACK TO NORMAL SOON.

WHAT'S **THAT?**

THIS?

JUST A CARD I MADE FOR NATE.

GET WELL SOON!!

YOU... THINK THERE'S A **MONSTER** IN THE BACKYARD?

I DON'T KNOW, BUT I **HAVE** TO GO LOOK!

NATE, HOW ABOUT THE TWO OF US CHECK IT OUT?

PERFECT!

YEAH!

I'LL GET MY CRUTCHES!

UM... I...MEANT **ELIJAH** AND ME.

OH.

BUT... WE'LL BE RIGHT BACK!

IT'LL BE AN **ADVENTURE**!

RIGHT, ELI?

RIGHT...

KRA-KOOM!

WAS THAT LIGHTNING?

COULD IT HAVE...?

DID IT...?

KRAK!

AHHH! AHHH! AHHHH!

76

MYSTERIES AND MALFUNCTIONS

BIG BANSHEE'S BOG (AKA SOPHIE'S BASEMENT)...

ALRIGHT, TEAM, HOW ARE WE GOING TO HUNT DOWN THIS **MONSTER**?

BECAUSE...

VIJAY THINKS IT'S HUNTING **HIM**.

SO... THAT'S THE THING.

I'M...

I'M NOT SURE IT'S **REALLY** A MONSTER AT ALL.

THE SEARCH CONTINUES! SUSPECTS #2 AND #3: **PETER** AND **ROY**

AH HA!

WE'VE **CAUGHT** YOU **RED-HANDED!!**

OR TECHNICALLY...

RED- AND ALSO **GREEN-**HANDED!!

HEY!

HANDS OFF MY HENCHMEN!

GREETINGS. THE ROBOT REVOLUTION BEGINS.

IT'S NOT FINISHED, BUT... I'VE DONE A LOT OF WORK ON IT!

JUST IN CASE YOU WANT TO GO TRICK-OR-TREATING WITH... **DADBOT**?

THANKS, DAD.

I MEAN...

I MEAN...

THANK YOU, PARENTAL UNIT.

I NEED TO GO NOW.

THAT EVENING...

SETH?

ARE YOU WATCHING OUT FOR THE MONSTER?

YUP! AND SPEEDY IS HELPING.

HE'S IN HIS NEW COSTUME!

I CALL HIM "GAR-DOG"!

LIKE... "GARGOYLE" PLUS "DOG," RIGHT?

AND IT ALSO SOUNDS LIKE "GUARD DOG"!

WHOA, YOU'RE RIGHT!

HA HA!

SHIKHA, HAVE YOU **TALKED** TO VIJAY ABOUT HIS FEELINGS?

YOU KNOW, REALLY **LISTENED** TO HIM?

KIND OF.

I TOLD HIM I'D **FIX** EVERYTHING.

BUT, SHIKHA, EVEN WHEN WE FIND THE MONSTER, VIJAY MIGHT **NOT** BE OKAY.

IT'S NOT GOING TO MAGICALLY **FIX** EVERYTHING.

I KNOW.

I JUST...

I JUST WANT TO **STOP** THIS STUPID MONSTER AND WHOEVER MADE IT.

WHEN I WAS SAD LAST SUMMER, I TALKED TO MY MOM ABOUT IT.

SHE COULDN'T **FIX** EVERYTHING, BUT SHE WAS **THERE** FOR ME.

SHE **LISTENED**.

MAYBE THAT'S WHAT VIJAY NEEDS, TOO.

BUT...

I...

I GUESS YOU'RE RIGHT.

ELIJAH!!

HUH?

WAKE UP!

EVERYONE'S DOWNSTAIRS!

MIGUEL?

COME ON!

NATE CALLED AN **EMERGENCY MONSTER MASHER MEETING** BEFORE SCHOOL.

IT'S...**BAD.**

BUT...

BUT I HARDLY GOT ANY SLEEP.

WHAT'S GOING ON?

SOMEONE **FOUND** SOMETHING.

A CLUE.

A...A PIECE OF THE **MONSTER.**

WHAT?!

HEY, KIDDOS, YOUR BUS IS HERE!

YOU'D BETTER HURRY OUT THERE!

BUT, DAD, WE BARELY STARTED!

OH, DON'T WORRY!

WE'LL GET RIGHT BACK TO WORK AFTER SCHOOL!

BUT THERE'S SO MUCH TO DISCUSS!

INDEED!

THE MISSING WAGON, THE MONSTER'S PATH, THE...

BYE, NATE!

I JUST...

I FEEL LIKE IT'S ALL CONNECTED.

...SOMEHOW.

MONSTER
SIGHTING
—VIJAY

MAPS AND TRAPS

HEY, ALICE?

SNIFF

I'M **NOT** CRYING!

OKAY.

THEY DON'T **UNDERSTAND** HOW THE WORLD **WORKS**!

IT'S **EAT** OR BE **EATEN**!

HEY, YOU KNOW WHAT **I** DO WHEN I'M UPSET?

I GO TO THE PARK AND THROW STUFF IN THE CREEK!

WANNA TRY?

MAYBE I SHOULD HEAD TO THE PARK BEFORE--

WHAT'S AT THE **PARK**?

UH...

WHAT'S ALL **THIS**?

IT'S ALL THE MONSTER SIGHTINGS!

WOW!

BRILLIANT!

I WAS JUST TELLING MIGUEL--

WE THINK THE MONSTER MIGHT BE IN THE PARK!

RIGHT, MIGUEL?

...MIGUEL?

HI, ELIJAH!

WHAT? OH, HI.

WOULD YOU LIKE TO SEE OUR MONSTER TRAPS? THEY--

AMANDA?

HAS ONE OF YOUR EXPERIMENTS EVER TURNED **EVIL** AND **HURT** PEOPLE AND TERRORIZED **EVERYONE YOU KNOW AND LOVE**?!

HMM...

NO, I DON'T **THINK** SO.

LET ME LOOK AT MY LAB NOTES FOR ANYTHING THAT...

ELIJAH?

I'M SORRY, NATE.

THE MONSTER...

IT WASN'T IN THE PARK.

REALLY? YOU LOOKED **EVERYWHERE**?

THE POND, THE PLAYGROUND, THE CREEK?

YEAH, OF COURSE.

BUT...

DANG. I WAS **SURE** THAT IT WOULD BE THERE.

I GUESS I DON'T KNOW AS MUCH AS I **THINK** I DO.

NATE, DON'T...

WE'RE GETTING **CLOSE**, I CAN **FEEL** IT.

AND...

AND I'LL DO EVERYTHING I CAN TO HELP YOU FIND IT.

I PROMISE.

ARE YOU GUYS **HUNGRY**?

WANT SOME COOKIES?

BEFORE DINNER??

THAT'S NOT ALLOWED!

TODAY... I'LL ALLOW IT.

FOR I AM **SHIKHA**, HUNTER OF **MONSTERS**, GUARDIAN OF **COOKIES**!

HERE YOU GO!

OH! AND I'LL GET YOU SOME **MILK**!

OH!

HEY! ALICE!

WHAT DO YOU WANT, BECKY?

ARE YOU DOING OKAY?

OF COURSE, I'M **ALWAYS** OKAY.

I'M **BETTER** THAN OKAY.

I'M ABSOLUTELY **GREAT**.

WELL, UM, GOOD!

I WAS...

I WAS JUST **WORRIED** ABOUT YOU.

WORRIED?? **WHY**?

UMMMMMM, YOU KNOW.

EARLIER?

I THINK YOU CAN TAKE THINGS **WAY TOO FAR** AND...

IT'S SORT OF HARD ON YOUR FRIENDS.

WHAT, LIKE **YOU**?

THE "FRIEND" WHO **FIRED** ME?

I **DIDN'T** FIRE YOU!! **YOU'RE** THE ONE WHO--

IT DOESN'T MATTER, ANYWAY.

I'VE **MOVED ON** TO BETTER THINGS.

OH?

YES.

CONSIDER THIS A "FRIENDLY" WARNING--

YOUR **HAUNTED GARAGE** DOESN'T STAND A **CHANCE** AGAINST WHAT **I'M** WORKING ON.

MWAHAHAHA!!!!

THE
NIGHT
GUARD

AAAGHH!

WAS THAT THE...?

IT'S THE **MONSTER**!!

EVERYONE!!

IT'S **HERE**!!

CLOSE THE DOOR, NATE!

IT'S **NOT SAFE**!

DON'T GO OUT THERE!!

ELIJAH...

PLEASE DON'T.

PLEASE.

WHERE'D IT **GO**?

AROUND THE CORNER!

IT'S **FAST**!

LET'S GET IT, MONSTER MASHERS!

DO **YOU** KNOW WHAT'S GOING ON, MIGUEL?

NOT AT **ALL**!

HMM.

WHOOO!! GOOD LUCK, SHIKHA!!

I **DON'T**! YOU HAVE TO **TRUST** ME!

THE MAGICAL MORNING

UM. IT **IS** HALLOWEEN, RIGHT?

ISN'T ANYONE ELSE WEARING A **COSTUME** TO SCHOOL?

I DON'T THINK ANYONE'S IN THE MOOD FOR THAT, JACK.

BECAUSE OF LAST NIGHT? WITH THE MONSTER?

THE KINGDOM ISN'T **SAFE**.

A LOT OF US ARE WORRIED.

HAPPY HALLOWEEN, EVERYONE!

WE JUST WANTED TO LET ALL OF YOU KNOW...

PETER, ROY, AND I **WILL** BE OPENING OUR HAUNTED HOUSE TONIGHT! FOR **FREE**!

WE CREATED **SO MUCH** COOL CARDBOARD STUFF, AND WE'RE EXCITED TO SHARE IT!

WE DIALED BACK SOME OF ALICE'S MORE...QUESTIONABLE CHOICES, SO IT WILL BE LOTS OF FUN!

YEAH, IT'S STILL SCARY, BUT...NOT **ALICE**-SCARY.

HA!

SOUNDS ADORABLE.

WELL...

SPEAK OF THE DEVIL.

AFTER SCHOOL...

WAIT.

WAS THAT **ALICE** LAST NIGHT?

CONTROLLING THE MONSTER?

HUH?

WHAT DO YOU MEAN?

IT WAS A **STUNT**!

TO KEEP US **SCARED** OF THE MONSTER AND SELL TICKETS TO HER SHOW!

SO YOU THINK SHE **STAGED** THE MONSTER SIGHTING TO **BUILD BUZZ** ABOUT IT?

WOULD SHE REALLY **DO** THAT?

I THINK SHE **WOULD**.

THE QUESTION IS:

WHAT DO **WE** DO ABOUT IT?

WHERE DO YOU THINK SHE'S GOT IT?

WHERE'S SHE HIDING THE MONSTER?

I DON'T KNOW...

BUT I'M GOING TO FIND OUT.

IT'S... IT'S NOT GOING TO BE **DANGEROUS**, IS IT?

NO, DON'T WORRY, VIJAY.

BUT, MIGUEL... **I'M** WORRIED. ABOUT **ALL** OF THIS.

I... ME TOO.

HEY! ALICE!!

SORRY, ADVANCE TICKET SALES ARE OVER.

WE'LL ANNOUNCE THE SECRET LOCATION OF THE MONSTER'S LAIR TONIGHT.

YOU CAN BUY TICKETS AT THE DOOR.

IT'S **NOT** RIGHT.

WHAT YOU **DID** LAST NIGHT, ALICE.

WHAT I **DID**?

I DID WHAT NONE OF **YOU** COULD DO--

I MASTERED THE **MONSTER!**

AND **NOW** I CAN DO **WHATEVER** I WANT WITH IT.

MEANWHILE...

UGH, I'VE GOT TO REDO MY MAKEUP FOR TONIGHT.

WHEN DO YOU WANT TO GO TRICK-OR-TREATING?

OH, I CAN'T GO, JACK.

WHAT?

WHAT ARE YOU **TALKING** ABOUT?!

I HAVE TO HELP ALICE WITH THE **BIG EVENT!**

THE **MONSTER REVEALED!**

IT'S GONNA BE **AWESOME!**

BUT... ISN'T TRICK-OR-TREATING WITH **ME** AWESOME?

YEAH, BUT, I MEAN...

SLAM!

JACK!!

FINE, FINE, DO **WHATEVER** ALICE DEMANDS!

I JUST THOUGHT YOU WERE **DONE** BEING ANYONE ELSE'S **MINION!**

THAT'S **NOT--**

ACROSS THE KINGDOM...

WE'RE **NOT** BUYING YOUR TICKETS, ALICE.

IS THIS... IS THIS A **BOYCOTT**??

BUT I'VE GOT THE **MONSTER**! THE ONE YOU'VE ALL BEEN OBSESSED WITH!

EXACTLY, ALICE.

VIJAY HAS BARELY **SLEPT** ALL WEEK!

HE'S BEEN SCARED TO **LEAVE** THE **HOUSE**!

AND YOU'RE TRYING TO **CASH IN** ON THAT?

BUT... IT'S...

THIS NEEDS TO **END**.

YOU SEE THAT, DON'T YOU?

I... I SEE.

HOW CAN I **FIX** THIS?

I WANT YOU TO TAKE US TO IT.

I WANT TO **MEET** THE **MONSTER**.

DAD!

I NEED TO GO OUTSIDE!

I'M MISSING A MONSTER MASHER MEETING!

WHAT?

THEY NEED ME!

AND I...

I NEED TO...

HUH?

ELIJAH MADE THE MONSTER?

DID **YOU** KNOW?

UM...

BUT WHAT **IS** THE MONSTER?

YEAH, I DON'T UNDERSTAND WHAT IT'S SUPPOSED TO **BE**.

YOU DON'T GET IT? **NONE** OF YOU?

I DO, ELIJAH!

I KNOW IT'S NOT **FINISHED**, BUT...

I DIDN'T THINK IT WOULD BE SO HARD TO **SEE**.

I SEE IT, ELI.

IT'S **MISSING** SOMETHING.

HERE.

OH!

THE PIECE THAT TORE OFF!

I GUESS... I'M FINALLY PUTTING THE PIECES TOGETHER.

NOW DO YOU SEE IT?

IT'S **ME**!

IT'S...
THE BEAST!

NATE!!

STOP, MIGUEL! **DON'T** DISAPPEAR AGAIN!

BUT...

YOU'VE BEEN DOING THAT **WAY TOO MUCH.**

I JUST... I...

I DON'T KNOW WHAT TO **DO**, NATE!

OR WHAT TO **SAY**!

HOW WILL YOU EVER **FORGIVE** ME?

ELIJAH TOLD ME **EVERYTHING**, MIGUEL.

I THINK EVERYTHING'S FINISHED, NATE!

NICE WORK, EVERYONE!

THE BEAST IS AN IMPORTANT PART OF MY PLAN.

YOU... YOU HAVE A **PLAN**, NATE?

TO **STOP** THOSE TERRIBLE TEENS?

I...

I **DO**!

BRUTE FORCE WON'T WORK AGAINST THEM!

THEY JUST **LAUGHED** AT US!

AND **ALSO** THEY THREW PUMPKINS!

THEN IT'S TIME FOR... A **DIFFERENT** APPROACH.

SCRIBE, DO YOU HAVE MAPS OF THE NEIGHBORHOOD?

OF COURSE!

SCIENCE SQUAD, DO YOU STILL HAVE THOSE TRAPS?

WE DO!

EVERYONE, ARE YOU READY?

YES!

AFFIRMATIVE.

DEFINITELY!

WHAT ABOUT **YOU**, VIJAY?

ARE **YOU** READY TO FACE THE TEENS AGAIN?

IS THE **BEAST** READY?

ROARR!

STINKIEST SLIME IN THE WORLD

THE KID'S MAGIC TRICK--

THAT'S WHAT THIS **IS**!

WE'VE BEEN **TRICKED**!

LILY, I...

IT WAS ALL A BIG **PRANK**?

IT WAS SERIOUSLY JUST SOME **KIDS** AND **CARDBOARD**?

OH MAN, I'M GONNA--

GRRRRRR

WAIT, THAT'S **YOU?**

THE... LITTLE KITTY CAT?

HE'S NOT SO LITTLE ANYMORE, IS HE?

NO, THAT'S AN AWESOME COSTUME!

I'M, UH...

I'M SORRY I GAVE YOU A HARD TIME BEFORE.

ARE WE COOL?

NO, WE ARE **NOT** COOL!

UH-OH, BIG SISTER'S IN BEAST MODE AGAIN...

YOU **BET** I AM!

VIJAY'S BEEN A WRECK ALL WEEK BECAUSE OF **YOU!**

HE DOESN'T HAVE TO FORGIVE YOU FOR **ANYTHING.**

YOU...

YOU DIDN'T **HAVE TO** STAY UP HERE WITH ME, MIGUEL.

YOU COULDN'T HAVE MADE IT DOWN THERE ON YOUR CRUTCH, NATE.

BUT YOU **MISSED OUT** ON ALL THE **FUN** STUFF DOWN THERE.

"FUN"?

NOTHING ABOUT THIS WEEK HAS BEEN **FUN**.

WHAT DO YOU **MEAN**?

YOU KNOW...

WITH YOUR LEG, THE **MONSTER**...

SO MANY SECRETS...

AND...**LIES**...

THIS MUST BE THE **WORST** HALLOWEEN **EVER**.

WELL, I DON'T THINK SO.

IN **MY** OPINION...

IT'S BEEN... **PERFECT**.

HAL LOW EEN

HOW WE BUILT THE KINGDOM

The Cardboard Kingdom: Roar of the Beast represents the collaborative efforts of nine different writers' work in partnership with Chad Sell, who led the project and illustrated the book. Over the course of countless phone calls, the creators sketched out their ideas for an epic Halloween mystery and then split into teams to tackle the various interweaving storylines in *Roar of the Beast*. Each collaborator primarily took responsibility for writing the scenes involving the characters they originally contributed to the Cardboard Kingdom series, which are outlined below.

JAY FULLER

Jack the Sorceress, Sam the Goblin & Peter

Jay is a cartoonist living in Brooklyn, New York, with his husband, Kevin, and their little corgi pup, Darwin. He writes and illustrates his comic, *The Boy in Pink Earmuffs*. Jay is inspired by his own childhood adventures growing up in Rhode Island, as well as the boundless creativity of his young nieces, Lillie and Kyla, and his nephew, Ray.

DAVID DEMEO

Shikha the Huntress, Vijay the Beast & Roy the Bully

David is a bald jewelry designer with a very large variety of hats. His favorite holiday is Halloween, and even though he is supposedly a grown-up now, he still makes his own costumes every year. David lives in Caldwell, New Jersey. The Huntress is based on David's babysitting responsibilities as the oldest of three beast brothers.

KATIE SCHENKEL
Sophie the Big Banshee

Katie Schenkel writes lots of kids' graphic novels, including *The Wolf in Unicorn's Clothing*, *My Slime Is Alive!*, and *Alice, Secret Agent of Wonderland*. A lifelong fan of superheroes, she had so much fun creating her own superhero team in the Big Banshee, the Huntress, and the Knight! Katie lives in Chicago with her partner, Madison.

MANUEL BETANCOURT
Nate the Prince & Miguel the Rogue

Manuel spends his days writing, baking, and watching way too many films and TV shows. He's the author of *Judy at Carnegie Hall* (2020). Manuel is happy to have gotten the chance to go on yet another adventure with the Prince and the Rogue, two boys who are very dear to his heart and who were inspired by his own childhood love of animated fairy tales.

MOLLY MULDOON
The Animal Queen

Molly is a writer, editor, and newly minted librarian who's always on the move with her pawtner-in-crime, Jamie McKitten. At the moment, they live in Portland, Oregon. The Animal Queen was inspired by Molly's childhood menagerie of stuffed animals.

VID ALLIGER

Elijah the Blob & Connie the Robot

Vid is an artist and writer currently living in Los Angeles. He loves everything about Halloween, but his favorite parts are the costumes and the candy. He is so grateful to have had the opportunity to work with so many wonderful, creative people on another adventure in the Cardboard Kingdom.

CLOUD JACOBS

Professor Everything

Cloud is a fifth-grade teacher in Stuttgart, Arkansas. When he's not reading and writing comics, he's working his way through every Star Wars book he can get his hands on. Professor Everything is based on Cloud's awkward childhood, when he would usually be reading while the other kids were playing football.

MICHAEL COLE

The Gargoyle

Michael is a faculty member in the English department at Wichita State University, where he teaches literature courses in horror fiction and LGBTQ+ literary representation. He spends most of his free time playing with his dogs, Hal, Atlas, and Benny. He still wants to be Jean Grey but wouldn't mind being a gargoyle either.

BARBARA PEREZ MARQUEZ

The Mad Scientist

Barbara is a Dominican American writer. She lives in Baltimore and has been writing since she was in seventh grade. Just like Amanda, Barbara was born and raised in the Dominican Republic, loves mustaches, and believes we can all experiment a little more in life!

KRIS MOORE

Kris Moore contributed the characters Alice the Alchemist and Becky the Blacksmith, who both appeared in the first book of the Cardboard Kingdom series. Kris passed away before the first installment was published, but his partner, Weston, has permitted us to continue Alice's and Becky's adventures. We're honored that Kris's memory lives on through the unforgettable characters he created and shared with all of us.

COSTUME DESIGN FOR
ROAR OF THE BEAST

Wardrobe change! Volume one of the Cardboard Kingdom series was set during the summer. Here's how Chad Sell updated many of the characters' clothes for autumn in *Roar of the Beast*.

COVER GALLERY

These sketches were alternate cover concepts for
The Cardboard Kingdom: Roar of the Beast!

To my husband, Dan
—C.S.

THIS IS A BORZOI BOOK PUBLISHED BY ALFRED A. KNOPF

This is a work of fiction. Names, characters, places, and incidents either are the product
of the authors' imagination or are used fictitiously. Any resemblance to actual persons,
living or dead, events, or locales is entirely coincidental.

Text copyright © 2021 by Chad Sell, Vid Alliger, Manuel Betancourt,
Michael Cole, David DeMeo, Jay Fuller, Cloud Jacobs, Barbara Perez Marquez,
Molly Muldoon, and Katie Schenkel

Jacket art and interior illustrations copyright © 2021 by Chad Sell

All rights reserved. Published in the United States by Alfred A. Knopf, an imprint of
Random House Children's Books, a division of Penguin Random House LLC, New York.

Knopf, Borzoi Books, and the colophon are registered trademarks of
Penguin Random House LLC.

RH Graphic with the book design is a trademark of Penguin Random House LLC.

Visit us on the Web! rhcbooks.com

Educators and librarians, for a variety of teaching tools,
visit us at RHTeachersLibrarians.com

Library of Congress Cataloging-in-Publication Data is available upon request.
ISBN 978-0-593-12554-0 (hardcover) — ISBN 978-0-593-12555-7 (pbk.) —
ISBN 978-0-593-31024-3 (lib. bdg.) — ISBN 978-0-593-12556-4 (ebook)

The illustrations were created using Clip Studio Paint.
Book design by Chad Sell and Sylvia Bi

MANUFACTURED IN CHINA
June 2021
10 9 8 7 6 5 4 3 2 1
First Edition

Random House Children's Books supports the First Amendment
and celebrates the right to read.